Text copyright © 2023 by **Ksenia Valakhanovich**
Illustrations copyright © 2023 by **Mary Koless**

First published in the United States of America in January 2024 by "Clever-Media-Group" LLC
www.clever-publishing.com
CLEVER is a registered trademark of "Clever-Media-Group" LLC

ISBN 978-1-954738-67-6 (hardcover)

For information about permission to reproduce selections from this book, write to:

CLEVER PUBLISHING
79 MADISON AVENUE; 8TH FLOOR
NEW YORK, NY 10016

For general inquiries, contact: info@clever-publishing.com
CLEVER is a registered trademark of "Clever-Media-Group" LLC

To place an order for Clever Publishing books, please contact The Quarto Group:
sales@quarto.com • Tel: (+1) 800-328-0590

Art created digitally
Book design by Katerina Belyaeva
MANUFACTURED, PRINTED, AND ASSEMBLED IN CHINA

10 9 8 7 6 5 4 3 2 1

by KSENIA VALAKHANOVICH

illustrated by MARY KOLESS

I Love You,
Honey Bunny

CLEVER
Publishing

I love you, Bunny, to the moon,
beyond the tallest pine.
I love you so much, all year round —
I'm so happy that you're mine!

SNOW ANGEL #1

SNOW ANGEL #2

FOR GIFTS

I love to spend my days with you, playing in the snow.

On warm and lazy summer days,
I watch you kick a ball.
Seeing all the fun you have
is the greatest joy of all.

On rainy days, we look at all
the fun things we have done.
Our pictures tell the sweetest tales —
I show you every one!

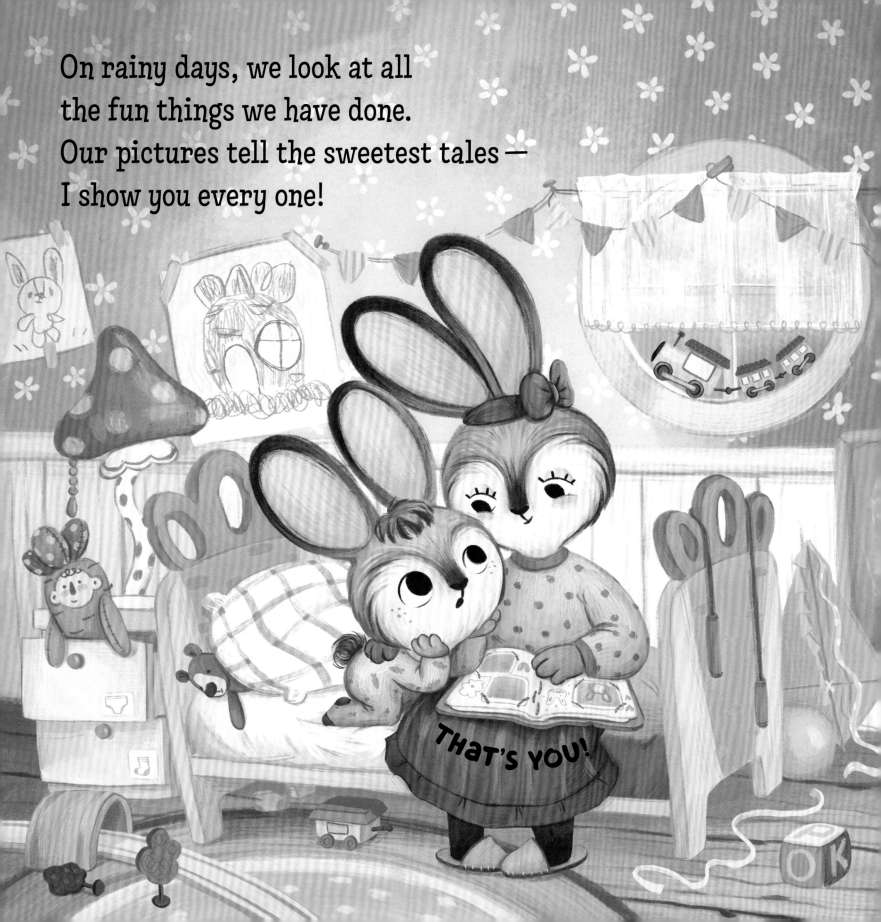

WAITING FOR THE TOOTH FAIRY

COOKING IS FUN!

I love to spend time in our yard,
doing chores and playing, too.
You find the perfect hiding spot —
peekaboo! I found you!

YOU'RE ALL DIRTY!

As you dig and scoop and build,
I watch you from inside.
Your careful planning makes me smile;
my heart is filled with pride.

Whenever you're not feeling well,
I'll take good care of you.

SPLASH! SPLASH!

And at Christmas, it's so much fun to decorate our place!

On your special day, my dear,
we celebrate and sing.
I just love to watch you smile —
you are my everything!

You love to help in summertime,
spraying water everywhere.
In fall, we like to trick-or-treat;
I love these times we share!

In spring, we plant some flowers
in special boxes on the ground.

SWISH

And when you're busy doing crafts,
you focus without a sound!

I love to watch you as you grow,
getting taller every day,

and wrap you in your favorite towel in my own special way.

When it's time to say good night,
you share your books with me.
We wish upon a falling star —
I'm right where I want to be.

When the morning sun appears,
we like to exercise!

We watch the forest wake from sleep
right before our eyes.

When it's warm, we take our tent
and camp under the trees.
We love to fish and play with toys
and feel the gentle breeze.

Honey Bunny, I love you—
you are my brightest star.
I'll always be right by your side,
no matter where you are!